This is a story that reveals how one tells the truth once and at other times may lies. It depends on his/her intention. Also, one can have a great effect on other peoples, by using his/her words; so words must be carefully picked, as they cost a lot when others misunderstand them—because the impact of words is very powerful.

I dedicate this work to my late and great mother, my beloved father, my husband and my kids, my sisters and to my brothers.

Najwan Mirza

THE IMPACT OF WORDS

AUSTIN MACAULEY PUBLISHERS™

LONDON • CAMBRIDGE • NEW YORK • SHARJAH

ISBN 9789948788959 (Paperback)
ISBN 9789948788942 (E-Book)

Application Number: MC-10-01-3147477
Age Classification: E

First Published 2023
AUSTIN MACAULEY PUBLISHERS FZE
Sharjah Publishing City
P.O Box [519201]
Sharjah, UAE
www.austinmacauley.ae
+971 655 95 202

To all those who believe in me and support me.

To my great family.

Thank you from the bottom of my heart. You are the stars that are shining in my life sky.

Introduction

This story shows the fact that, what is before you is not always the truth. The real truth can be revealed only when someone looks deep inside himself, and inside others. Then and only then, one can realize that people show truths and lies and we ourselves do the same with the difference of intentions.

The Impact of Words

Suzan is a very quiet, mild, tender, beautiful and compassionate girl. She adores flowers, all kinds and colours. Flowers everywhere outside her house. She is calm to the extent to be described as cold. Her mother, Sara, called her "miss silent" as words can barely come out her mouth. This even affected her charisma or that what it was thought about her.

"Mouth reveals much about people, of course not from its outside shape, but from the words come out." These are the teacher's wise words to the students. They naturally did not get their hidden meaning. Yet, there must be something within themselves, in their unconsciousness, that has been touched.

These deep words of the teacher are the required assignment. Which students have not only to write about at the end of the semester, but to convey their own experience about something that personally happened with them.

Suzan returned home and thought deeply about the report that she had to prepare, but how? She did understand the words apparently, yet did not know what to do. She tried to depend entirely on herself in this matter as it's her own real chance to do something or to prove something for herself. Within the family, although Suzan was the elder one, others took the lead in solving her problems whether they were serious or normal matters. Thinking of her disability to find a solution. In general, this affected her way of thinking while personally it affected her personality. She felt unsatisfied of what was happing around. It was maybe the family's job of over-protecting. It was actually not the family's fault as their role was to protect their beloved ones, neither hers that she grew up inside a family which do everything instead of her. She sometimes felt that she was unable to do anything even trivial things like choosing her dresses; she was chained, and if she did something wrong, she would be criticized or even grounded. She felt that she wanted to do many things but there was no way. She had her own style of doing things but sometimes parents did not understand that. Nevertheless, she had the right to try over and over again till knowing how, where and when she had to take the lead.

Suzan was somehow convinced that she could not do anything without the help of her mother. She always asked in spite of being fifteen-year-old as she was afraid of being blamed if she did not do well.

Each day, when Suzan went to school she was saw a sad boy near a house in the street behind her house, selling flowers which she described as the most beautiful flowers in the whole world. She became eager to know the boy's story and the reason behind that sad look. She did not know why, but maybe inside herself, she tried to search about a topic for her required assignment. Or who knows? Maybe she tried to find a topic for her life. So, she wanted to get to know his story by becoming close to him through buying a flower. In the beginning, she noticed that the boy had a deep wound on his forehead. He was always wearing a handmade woven hat with the letters (R. J. L) on it and was leaning his head toward the ground in order to hide his wound. Suzan tried to communicate with him, sometimes by saying, "good morning." Other times by smiling or even talking directly to him but all her efforts were in vain. He maintained his sad, and at times, angry look.

One day after her many attempts, when Suzan, dressed in her school clothes, went outside, she found at the doormat of the house a yellow flower. She took it, and placed it in her hair behind her ear. As she passed by, the boy looked at her with a slight smile drawn on his face. She said, "good morning." He said nothing. For a moment, she thought why she was even bothering herself by trying talking to him. He seemed arrogant and snobbish. Then she remembered her assignment and how she had to do something about it. So she was about to tell him her name but suddenly an old man appeared from his house and asked the boy for a sunflower. The boy made a nod as if he was used to granting that specific flower to that old man. Suzan then hurried to reach the school bus she was late. While she was running, she fell down—so the old man and the boy came to her quickly. The flower she was wearing, had been smashed. For that reason, the boy immediately gave her the same yellow lily rose. The old man looked at the boy and told him, "OK, nothing happened. Go to work now." Then, he looked at Suzan and said, "And you have to go to school."

Suzan looked at the boy with a sudden change in her feelings especially after knowing that he was the one who gave her the flower on the doormat. She felt that he tried to tell her something but that strange old man looked cruel somehow and prevented him from speak.

When she returned home after school, she wanted to see him but she did not know where he lived. She was used to seeing him in the morning on her way to school. So she took permission from her mother to go outside and to wander around the neighbourhood with her friends. In her mind, she really tried to find the mysterious boy and to talk to him. She even went to the old man's house (which was behind hers), to ask him about the boy's house. She knocked at the door twice, and then he appeared and was surprised to see her. Suzan told him that she tried to find the boy as she wanted to buy flowers from him. He told her, that the boy has no specific place. She wondered, "How come? Does anybody in the whole world have no home?" The old man answered her with a wise look, "Many my child, many!" (He meant something.) Then she asked about the boy's name and where could she find him.

The whole conversation happened outside the house. The old man said, "The boy does not want to speak and he forgets to listen."

The girl did not pay attention to the words; she continued her questions as if she just wanted to write about her assignment or just to prove something to herself.

"Do you know his story sir?" She asked.

He said, "Do you want me to narrate it to you?"

She answered, "Please do, if you do not mind."

"No, I think I do not mind. Let us start from the beginning. This boy was a very responsible kid. He had two sisters and his…"

She interrupted him and said surprisingly, "He *had* two sisters?" It seemed that she had started to listen.

He said, "Yes, my child, let me finish my speech."

"I am sorry sir, continue please," she said.

"His sisters were only 5 years old. His father was a farmer. So, Kris…"

She interrupted him again, "His name is Kris then!"

The old man said, "Yes, Kris. He used to go with his father to the field and as a hobby at first. He started to collect flower especially lilies and jasmine. But after a short time he became professional in knowing flowers and their various kinds along with other kinds of plants. One day, his father got sick with irremediable disease. For that reason, unfortunately, Kris took the lead from a very young age; he became responsible for feeding the whole family, when he was just 15 years old."

Suzan felt sorry for him with tears in her eyes and said, "Only fifteen he was?"

The old man answered, "Yes my dear, only fifteen."

She commented "He is too young to carry that burden on his shoulder."

"That is true," said the old man.

"Proceed sir, please; I would like to know the rest of the story," Suzan urged.

Abruptly, a sound of a thunder started, so he told her that she had to go home immediately as it seemed that it would rain heavily. The weather became so cold. He noticed her discontent as she tried to know the story. He promised that he would complete the story next day but she had to hurry up. Suzan returned home with a strong feeling that she had to finish listening to the old man's story. Then, she would write something extraordinary in her assignment. The next day, which was a holiday, Suzan found her same favourite flower on the doormat. She took it happily, and then she went in a hurry to the house of the old man after telling her mother that she would bring some stuff for her room. She knocked at the door more than once but there was no answer. Suddenly, when she was about to leave, the door opened. The old man was very sick because of the day they had spent outside. He had caught a cold. Suzan noticed that the old man's situation was not stable. He looked so tired. For that reason, she offered to help him enter the house. So, the old man leant against her. Through her way to go inside his house, she was amazed by the way his garden looked. She breathed different air, because of the fragrance of the various plants it had. It was a heavenly garden that possibly had every kind of colourful flower. While wandering inside the house to find the kitchen to make something warm for the old man, Suzan found a wall full of paintings. One of them, she noticed, belonged to the old man with a woman and two children (a girl and a boy). Below this painting 'THE FAMILY J&J' was written.

She made a cup of tea for him and excused immediately to go in order not to bother him since he needed rest. He told her that he felt better and thanked her for her kindness. He asked her to stay as he gave her a word to complete the story.

"Sir, is this your family?" She asked.

He answered with grief, "Yes this was my wife, she is my late wife and those are my children, and they were twins."

"I have twin brothers too," she commented.

The old man said with a low voice, "Yes I know." Suzan didn't understand what he meant.

Then she asked about his children, "Where are your children now?"

He did not answer her question but told her that he felt much better and was able to complete the story.

"Where were we, my child?" the old man inquired.

She answered, "Kris took the lead after his father's sickness."

The old man began to narrate, "Yes, now I remember. Kris becomes responsible for feeding the family. The hobby became the source for their living. Lily and jasmine – his two younger sisters – looked like angels. They were twins. He loved them so much but unfortunately he could not help them. They were allergic to something."

Suzan wondered "To what?" He answered that he did not know.

He continued "Kris knew what could make them better. It was special a kind of potion from rare flowers that must be mixed with other things to make the mixture to be used as an ointment."

Suzan said, "Oh God, healing the flowers by flowers… How nice!"

The old man answered, "No, it was not nice at all. Especially, that day." Then he stopped.

"What day, sir? Sir, what day? Please tell me what happened?" asked Suzan.

The old man remained silent nearly for three minutes as if he was remembering something that happened that day.

"Sir, are you all right? Would you like me to do something else for you?"

"No thank you. You are a good girl my dear. Your *mother* raised you well." (He stressed on mother.) He told her "You call me sir the whole time, I would prefer if you call me grandfather."

She smiled.

Then he continued, "I just want to sleep and it's better for you to go home, it is lunch time I guess. Your mother will be so worried about you. Come back at afternoon and then I will complete the story."

She returned home and found her mother worried about her. She apologized immediately and said nothing. At noon, Suzan's mother went to work. So it was a good chance for Suzan to go to the old man's house and to complete the story.

On her way to go to him, she found that the old man was walking in a hurry with his stick towards a long street. She followed him till they reached a farm. It was a very beautiful farm. She said, "I have never seen something like this."

"Why you are in a hurry, sir?" Suzan inquired.

"You have to tell me first, why you are following me?" the old man shouted at her.

She startled and said, "I am sorry, but I did not feel but my legs were following you as you told me that you would complete the story."

He apologized, "I am sorry, I am just worried about Kris. I haven't seen him for the last two days." Then the old man went to the cottage that Kris lived in and he found him in a deep sleep. So, quietly he withdrew and left Kris to have some rest…

On the way home, Suzan repeated her sorry and asked if she had done something wrong. She then demanded if he could continue with what had happened that night? The old man ordered her not to come here alone by herself. She promised not to do that.

He said, "Well then, where were we? I have become too old to remember by myself."

She said, "No, you are not old sir, but you are precise."

"You are a very polite girl, God bless you, Suzan," he said. She did not pay attention that he mentioned her name although she had not told him.

"Proceed Sir, we reached till *that day*. What happened that day?" she was looking forward to know what happened.

"Oh, you insist to call me sir?" he said. She was shy then said, "Yes grandfather complete your speech, please." He felt satisfied. He took a full breath then said, "That day, the weather was very bad. Yes, I remember it very well as if something sad was going to happen." The old man sat on a deck and leaned on his stick with a grief stricken look on his face towards the cottage and continued, "It was a dark night and a scary thunderstorm sound predicted something mighty. When Kris' two little sisters got really sick it was so cold and everything was gloomy. Kris went outside to bring some medicine but no one, of course, was out there. Nobody wanted to be killed. For that reason, the poor boy tried to collect the ingredients of the medicine by himself. So, he went far to find the main ingredients, to mix them in order to make his sisters feel better. Thereafter, Kris found a cliff filled with those flowers by the lightening of the thunder. Subsequently, he got up to bring them quickly."

Suzan said, "How brave he is! It is too dangerous to do such a thing."

The old man said, "Yes he was so brave. He reached the flowers and took some, but while getting off, his foot had slipped and something hit him hard on his forehead. Meanwhile, he was holding the flowers strongly on his hand."

"Ah, this is the reason of that wound!" Suzan linked events by talking to herself.

"So he fainted, and could not wake up till morning. The weather had gotten better. Sun had risen and rain had stopped. It seemed that on this ominous day something very bad would happen. Then, Kris walked back through the rocks with a strong headache till he reached home with his injured head and palm because of the pressure of holding the flowers."

Suzan said, "Oh, thank God, finally he made it."

"No my dear, Kris wished he never awakened that day."

"Why? What? What happened?"

He said with sorrow, "His sisters died."

Suzan shouted, "Died?" She began to cry hard. The old man apologized and told her that she insisted to complete the story. Then he inquired, "Why, my child, were you insisting to know Kris's story?"

She told him while she was crying, "Actually, I tried to know his story to write about it in my required assignment, then I saw some kindness in him." (When he gave her the flower at the doormat and after losing her flower he gave her another one as compensation). She continued "So I tried to pay back something from what he did to me. I think he spread happiness by selling flowers in spite of all what he went through. I thought I could help him but it seems impossible. Everything I do turn out to be improper," Suzan said with a deep grief.

The old man said confidently, "Nothing is impossible my dear, keep this in your mind, everything can be done with great patience and little wisdom. You are a good girl and what you are doing now shows your goodness but it is better to leave Kris alone. You must never talk to him," he strongly insisted. She promised him. At that moment, he relieved and took a deep breath, then he proceeded, "Do you want me to complete the story or you see that is enough and it is better to go home now?"

"No grandpa, please tell me more," she insisted because she was curios and eager to know what happened next.

"After that day, Kris blamed himself very much so he left the house and the whole town in order not to remember. And since that time he did not talk again." The old man ended his speech.

"Grandpa, may I ask you a question?" she asked while they were walking towards her home.

"Yes, of course," he answered.

"How did you know all this in detail?" Suzan interrogated.

"Oh, I guess I forgot to tell you that I am the owner of a factory which was used to produce perfumes and Kris's father was bringing flowers to that factory, so I knew Kris from his early childhood, when he would come with his father." Hesitantly, he added, "From that time onwards, we left our village and I took him to many places and our final destination is where we are now. I gave him one of my farms that I own, hoping to find some peace."

"Sir, how old is Kris now?" she asked.

"He is twenty-five years old." He answered.

"Oh, ten years… hmmm… the accident had happened when he was fifteen years old and the wound has not healed?"

The old man replied, "The fall was very severe to make that scar."

"Grandpa, I am sorry I did not mean the scar, I meant his heart wound."

He smiled and stated, "This is deep thinking from a fifteen-year-old girl. You are fifteen, right my dear?"

"Yes, I am." She did not know how he knew her real age but she thought it was just a guess.

"Thank you so much for taking out time for this conversation." she affirmed.

"Not at all, my dear but I hope that you will keep your promise by staying away from Kris."

He desired to be alone again, the old man insisted. Suzan sometimes became afraid of the old man's looks and words. As he seemed hot-tempered with sharp features once, and at other times he seemed generous and compassionate.

She returned home thinking deeply how could she help Kris. His story was very touching. Next morning, she went to school and during the rest period, she kept on thinking to visit the farm that Kris lived in. Before that, Suzan believed that she had to know extra information about Kris. Specifically, she wanted to know where his family is right now. And why they have not asked about him in all these years hoping she could reach them. So, she needed to go and ask the old man again. After school, she decided to go to the old man's house to ask him these questions. On her way, she found a woman breathing hardly, trying to take some rest (as she had to pull several bags with her). Suzan offered the woman to help. The woman thanked Suzan a lot and asked her if she could just help her to go to a nearby house. Suzan did not mind and walked with the woman to a house which, surprisingly, was the old man's house. Suzan knocked at the door and the old man welcomed her but not the other woman. After that, the old man told Suzan before she started talking "I do believe that this woman would be the answer for one of your questions Suzan, but not now."

She answered surprisingly, "This woman? I do not even know this woman."

He told her, "Well then, it is just you have only to remember her face." He turned and gazed at the woman and said, "As I guess, Suzan, you will never meet again as long as I live."

The woman looked at Suzan with astonishment. She tried to say something but something prevented her so she stayed silent with a look of hatred.

Suzan was about to leave, she tried to excuse herself as she did not understand what had just happened but the old man insisted her to stay. Near the fireplace sat the woman on a chair. She looked at the old man with many thoughts. Near the chair, there was a large bag. She opened it without saying a word. It contained clothes, hats, shoes and even money. Thereafter, she gave it to the old man. He was unsatisfied; his two hands were on his stick. His face expression was stuffy. He wanted her to leave quickly; he did not accept her money or even her existence. The woman looked at him, she was sad. Then, she looked at Suzan with a cold strange look. After that, she left the house with no words and the old man turned around towards the family painting in order not to see her while leaving. Suzan thought, *the woman seems as if she is used to come here.* That was obvious from the way the old man received her (as he recognized her quickly and let her enter the house without any reaction).

"I think Suzan; you have lots of questions right now. Am I right?" The old man asked gently.

She opened her two big beautiful eyes, smiled and said, "No sir, I do not want to intrude."

He replied, "Are you sure Suzan?"

She said, "Truly speaking sir. I am not sure I am dying to know who this is."

The old man laughed and said, "Ok then, that is Kris' mother."

"Oh, really! She is young and beautiful. I thought she might be old." Suzan said.

"No, she is not old. She got married to Kris' father at a very young age. Then after her husband's death, she got married to a very wealthy man," the old man replied.

"Uh! Now I understand everything," Suzan said confidently.

"Understand what, my child?" The old man smiled and said, "I do remember that I've told you that, this woman will be the answer for one of your questions but I also said that it is not now." He continued "You understand nothing. Believe me."

Suzan was not listening again and she continued her sequential questions. "Why she does not go to see him at the farm that he is living in? Why she comes here? Why Kris left his parents immediately after the accident. It was not their fault." She wanted to know everything, without paying attention to the real things that she was supposed to listen to. Again, it was not her fault for rushing things.

The old man started to explain, "Kris does not refuse to see his mother; he had a shock or a denial to the past. For this reason, his parents left him alone hoping that he finds inner peace and let him go with me. This is called sacrifice which few, if any, can really do it. " He seemed sarcastic in saying that while looking at the family painting on the wall.

"What do you mean, grandpa?"

"Nothing my dear, never mind. I am just glad to hear the word grandpa from you." He continued, "Now, you know everything about Kris and you have a great topic for your assignment, I guess. So, you need to leave, and never search about him again. And remember, you have to keep your promise to stay away from him. As I've told you, he prefers to be alone by himself." The old man insisted for a third time and she promised again.

The first thing that came to Suzan's mind after leaving the old man's house was that she had to help Kris in all possible ways. She didn't know when she was going to submit her assignment and now she had the intention of working on a real assignment of helping him. A person like him needed a lot of support. There must be a support given to that person. She was attached to his story so much so that she forgot to pay attention to her promise.

Suzan thought that she had to go to the farm and to give it a try to talk to Kris. She actually went to the farm under the pretence that she wanted some special flowers for her mother's birthday. She reached the farm with extreme difficulties, and tried to find him among all the grasses, flowers, trees and other great things. However, she could not. When she tried to return back, she got lost and became frightened. She started running quickly and one of her earring fell down while running. Then, she remembered what the old man had told her about not coming alone to that place.

Suddenly, Kris caught her and told her coldly, "It is better for you not to come alone here, it is dangerous." While she was listening to him, she forgot the panic and became happy because he talked. After that, she asked him some questions but he returned to his old nature of not talking. She began to describe the types of flowers that she wanted to take with her. When he was preparing her order, she asked him about his name, as if she did not know it. Still, no answer. She immediately said, "My name is Suzan, what is yours? Is it Kris?"

He coldly responded, "Suzan," then he laughed at her. She did not know why he was laughing and asked him about the reason. He answered by repeating her question, "What is your name? Is it Kris? That is really funny. You seem that you already know my name so why do you ask?"

"No, I do not. I think I heard it once from someone but I wanted to be sure." She quickly found an excuse to handle the situation that she put herself in.

"This is your order kid," he said with a slight smile. She answered, "I am not a kid, I am fifteen years old." He immediately leaned his face and asked her to go. She was confused. "I am sorry, did I say something wrong?"

"No you did not, but I hate this number. I said go!" He shouted.

Kris did not know that Suzan knew his story very well and did not know that she intended good. Suzan within herself felt that she made a mistake by reminding Kris of this number, because of his calamity which had happened at that age. So for that reason she tried to start another conversation to make him feel better.

She said, "How you could take care of all these beautiful plants. You are a hero."

He remained silent again. *It is obvious that I am indulging myself in things that I should not,* Suzan thought. She somehow was trying to apologize to him but it was in vain.

She felt sad as he was not responding to her. She really and hardly was trying to help him.

"I think, Suzan, it is better for you to go right now. Apparently you have a school and a *mother* to take care of and worry about you I guess."

She did not pay attention to his words, for the second time there was a stress the word *mother*. She was eager to tell him that he himself has a mother who really loved and worried too much about him but he seemed as if he casted her away. She truly tried to tell him that, but she could not as she did not want to lose the progress that she was making (by making him talk and communicate with her).

She herself did not know why he talked to her in the first place. Maybe, she thought that she reminded him of his little sisters who supposedly would be fifteen by now.

When Suzan tried to return home, she looked at the way that she had to get through so she remained standstill with a scared look on her face and a thumb between her teeth. She was really afraid to go back alone.

Kris looked at her with a strange scary look. Then he laughed again at this sight and told her, "You really make me laugh. I think I will take you home *kid*." And he stressed on *kid*. Kris seemed to enjoy his time with Suzan, who in turn was trying to work hard not for the assignment, but for what she believed in. Here, Suzan learned her first lesson which is, when she had to take the lead (that is what she thought) but another question arises, how? How can she help him? How can she pay back the beauty and peace he spread in spite of his pain? For this reason, she thought it would be wonderful to make others to participate in communicating with him in order to help him not to be alone, and to have a good influence on him.

Next day, Suzan hurried to go outside the house as she was sure that she would find her same favourite flower like every day. She went to school and one of the lessons that she and the students used to study, once each week, was Herbology. The lecturer told them that he would not be able to teach them in the second semester as he had to complete his higher studies in another town. For that reason, he made an announcement saying, "There will be a contest open for all those who find in themselves the ability to teacher Herbology".

The teacher also added, "So, anyone who has enough experience to teach that subject, will be given this special opportunity for this year (even without any college degree). Any person applying has to first pass the contest in order to be qualified to do the exam. For this, if you know anyone's father, mother, relatives or friend that is more than twenty-two years old, is invited if he/she has enough knowledge."

In the beginning, Suzan took this as transient matter since no one – she thought of those whom she knew – wanted this job. So, she returned home after school and found her mother waiting for her furiously. She told Suzan, "There was a boy here today. He brought this back for you!"

Suzan was surprised. "My earring… a boy? What did he look like, Mother?"

Sara answered with an angry tone, "You have to tell me that." Suzan took a minute to remember, and then she knew that on the day before when she went to find Kris, she lost her earring at the farm. After that, she told her mother about Kris and the whole story because she did not want to lie.

Sara became so furious and started to argue. "How could you do this? This is not like you. I always call you *miss silent* because of your calm personality. How could you do this without my knowledge? Why did you hide this entire thing from me? You know it is wrong. Who gave you the permission to do that? Me? Your father when he came? I do not think so, how dare you to do that?" Suzan tried more than once to explain the situation but her mother was not letting her. Continuing with her questions and blaming she said, "What about the rule do not talk to the strangers? You did not just break it, but even went to the man's place and entered his house. And you went to a farm alone. This behaviour is not accepted at all kid."

"Mother, please, I just want to…" Suzan tried to explain her situation but her mother interrupted her. "Discussion is over. Go to your room," her mother ended her speech.

"It was not a discussion Mother, it was a quarrel. You always treat me like a child. I always do the things you want and not I want. I always make matters that are not right in your opinion. I always try to share my ideas with you but you refuse, you do not understand me. I like to do many things but I am locked in a cage. I want to live my life not yours," Suzan said that with rage while she was crying heartily.

Sara, her mother, looked at her quite surprised, with eyes wide open. She did not believed what she just heard. Suzan went upstairs with tears on her cheeks. Sara sat on a hummock chair near the window she used to sit on and thinks. She looked at the earring. She was upset and sad angry and confused. Her husband was not there for the family sake. He was always busy with his factory of medical stuff outside the town and even if she needed him he would not be there. She was tired to bear all these responsibilities alone. Many ideas were inside her mind. How would she treat her elder daughter from now on? She was thinking about what her daughter had said earlier and what she had to do.

Then, after two days, when Sara came down, she had a real discussion with her daughter. She started to talk quietly with Suzan, "You have the right to experience life and to do many things; but what is not your right is to do them alone without my knowledge or my permission. I really do care about you so much, and my duty is to show you the right way from the wrong."

She continued, "Maybe you behaved like this because you thought that I will prevent you to do what you did. That is true. Listen to me my love; there are certain things in life you cannot think about or even imagine. I, as the source of your protection and guidance, have to take certain decisions on your behalf. That is my duty that is my job."

Suzan interrupted and said. "But Mommy, I have to try things by myself or else how can I learn if I did not try?" She continued, "I admit that I was wrong when I behaved like this, but I was sure, as usual you would object what I wanted to do."

Sara explained, "Suzan, what I am doing is just for your good. I am not refusing or just objecting to what you want to do but things you were or still choosing mostly bigger than your size and that is what I want you to know and to know it very well. I am trying to protect you. It is not the matter of just doing things to prove something for yourself. The real matter is what things are, the value of what you are doing. And always remember that you have a family which means support, love and life."

"I am sorry, Mom. I will always share you all my feelings and intensions. I will do it from now onwards. I now get what you mean," replied Suzan.

"My lovely Suzan I just want to tell you it is not and will not be a matter of parent's controlling; it's just family care and love."

After a big hag and emotional scene between them, Suzan went with her mother to make dinner. While preparing food Sara asked, "You did not tell me what the old man's name is?"

"I'd prefer to call him the wise man. He is so gentle and generous," Suzan said while wearing gloves and preparing salad. "He even lets Kris lives in one of his farms. He seems very rich."

Sara wondered. "Kris, you said, and the old man who lives in the street behind us?"

"Yes Mommy, do you know him? How a good person he is?" Suzan said.

"You are talking about whom?" Sara said with astonishment. "Who is a good person? The monster man?"

"Mom, I am talking about the old man who looks like…"

Suzan began to describe him and his place. Sara said confidently, "Well then, he is the same one whom I am talking about."

"What do you mean by the monster, Mom?" Suzan startled and seemed pale.

"Listen darling, more than ten years ago, I cannot remember the exact time, an accident happened to the villagers who were living in a very wonderful place, rounded with great nature. There was a man who was very obsessive about planting all kinds of plants and flowers in his farms.

This person had a factory which he used for mixing plants with each other for the sake of producing ointments and for other medical stuff besides perfumes of Jasmine, Lily with others expensive ones to sell them in and outside the village. He was so greedy."

Suzan was watching and waiting for the connection between the old man, Kris and her mother's story.

Sara continued, "So one day, he ordered his workers to gather very dangerous kinds of plants, hoping they would give best results although of his knowledge he knew that mixing those flowers would be very dangerous as he was expert. He knew it would produce chemical substances. I do not remember his name; they mentioned it in the newspaper." Sara was talking to herself as she tried to remember it. "However, he probably used a large amount of them. For that reason, it became lethal which made some people in that village sick and some others were died."

Still Suzan was waiting with dishes in her hands.

"That greedy man, the old man at that time, was out of the city with his grandson, Kris, who had two other sisters who got sick and died. Also, Kris' father got very sick after that accident. This is what your father had mentioned to me once as he worked in that factory at that time."

She continued without paying attention to Suzan. "At that time we were living near that village. After knowing that the old man was responsible for that disaster, Kris' mother (the old man's daughter) prevented the old man to see his grandson again. Finally, after the death of the father, the old man took Kris from his daughter by obliging her to give up on him. Then, they settled down here."

Sara was smiling wondering how her chatty neighbour loved gossip as she told her that Kris' mother still came here and visit her in her house and complained about what the old man was still doing and how he treated her badly.

All of a sudden, Suzan fainted and the dishes crashed on the floor. When she awoke, she said nothing but her eyes were full of tears. *How could the old man deceive her by making up his story?* How she believed him. Many ideas come to her mind at that time and she was confused. Her scattered thoughts made her unable to think of what she had to do from now on. She was lying on her bed incurious of her health. Meanwhile, Sara took her to the doctor who told her that Suzan has an allergy to latex and she was to stay away from things that contain latex (It was in the gloves she was wearing when making salad. Her father brought a large amount of them with him from his factory in his last visit.)

Suzan was thinking deeply about what she had started. *Will she be able to complete it, or she has to ignore the whole thing.* She kept on remembering the whole speech that took place between the old man and her; comparing events, his way of conveying the whole fabricated story, and his insistence of staying away from Kris and not to help him. How he isolated him from people. She decided that whatever it took, she would complete the story and she herself would put an end to it. As she became fully aware, that her real assignment right now was saving Kris from the tyrant of a man.

Suzan asked Sara about Kris' mother (when she was remembering the whole thing and how the old man insisted that Suzan and Kris' mother will not meet again as long as he lives). Sara said, "I know nothing about his mother and what happened to her after that but once I heard my gossip neighbour mentioning how his father hated her so much because she got married without his acceptance. After her husband's death he took his grandson forcefully."

"OK Mother, now I know why he looked at her that day with so much hatred and never talked to her while she was in a desperate need to communicate with him but he totally rejected her. Poor woman. I also guessed he prevented her from seeing her own son. Everything is clear to me right now. I think, after your permission, Mom, I will help this person. He is deceived, Mother. He thinks, he has a good grandfather but it seems he knows nothing."

Sara kept silent for a moment and thought that her daughter was eager so if she refused what Suzan wanted she will harm her feelings and at the same time Suzan will behave in the opposite direction. So to keep her in front of her eyes she said, "You have my permission Suzy; always keep on doing good things but also be careful. And remember you have me all the time."

Replied Suzan, "OK, Mom, I will. Thank you."

At school, when posters were pasted on the sign-board concerning the contest of Herbology, an idea came to Suzan's mind. She needed to go to Kris one more time to tell him about that contest. As he was really good at that job. He had a great experience in it and had a real chance to win. So, after school she went to the farm in order to tell him about the idea. When she entered the farm, she found the old man talking to Kris. So she quickly hid and tried to hear them. She heard the old man saying, "Hear me Kris, I raised you and I took care of you when your mother abandoned you. I taught you everything regarding life and nature. Leave what you are thinking about. It is not right. Let it go Kris, let it go. Now is the time to show me what I've taught you in all these years. Do not listen to your mother. Her words are like poison." He shouted at Kris. Kris remained silent but seemed touched. The old man continued, "Do not make me regret everything. I will always be watching you as long as I live. Stay away from her. Stay away from them."

Suzan wished at that moment to hit that cruel man on his face, but she remained patient and took the wise decision to hold on and to wait till he left. After that, she tried to withdraw, as it was not the right time to talk about her subject with Kris but she stepped on a stick and made a sound. For this reason, Kris found her and asked her about the time she had been there. She told him about the speech she heard.

"How dare you enter here without my acceptance." He kept on insulting her "What an annoying, intruding and provoking girl."

She started crying. He immediately apologized and asked her about the reason behind her visiting. She asked, "May I know first, what is the reason behind that argument between the old man and you." He thought for a moment and replied that he told him about his desire to complete his study but he did not accept. Then he again asked her, "Why have you come here, Suzan?"

Suzan felt that she needed more time before telling him about the contest, as she thought Kris will face a big problem with his grandfather if he knew about the contest. Because she was convinced that he wanted to isolate his grandson from any contact and this was assured by the speech she had heard between them shortly before.

So, she told him about her allergy as she tried to find an excuse for her coming. Due to being an expert in this field "I want to take your advice about things that I have to be close to, or to stay away from. As it seems that I have an allergy from latex."

"What?" Kris asked surprised. "From what you say? From latex?"

"Did you not hear me?" Suzan asked.

"Of course, I heard. But I just want to be sure of what I have heard. " As if days were repeating themselves. "I will give you a special kind of plant as a present Lily. (He said his sister's name; he remembered her.) It will make you much better. I am sure of it. Put it in your room, it will help you so much." While Kris was giving Suzan the plant, he told her while gazing at it with eyes full of tears that he spent most of his life taking care and planting many flowers and other things but he could not save those whom he loved.

Suzan immediately changed her mind and decided to tell him about the contest as she was sure that this matter will make him feel happy. For that reason, she thanked him a lot for the generous gift and when she tried to tell him about the contest, she sneezed loudly. He smiled and said, "God bless you."

After that he told him about the contest and convinced him to participate. He seemed excited about it and asked her about the time and the things that he had to study and prepare. She said that she would help him in getting all the information that he needed with the help of her friends.

When she returned home, she felt that she was not all right. She thought to herself, *I think that I am sick.* She put the gift that her friend Kris had given her in the corner and fell asleep. Then she saw a nightmare:

"Hi Suzan."

"Hi, little angels. Who are you?"

"I am Lily and I am Jasmine. We came to take you with us."

Suddenly, Suzan woke up screaming. Sara rushed to reach her quickly and told her that it was just a nightmare. Suzan felt extremely frightened and asked her mother to go with her to her room. So, they went to her mother's room and when Sara was trying to bring a scarf for Suzan from the cupboard, accidently an old box of pictures fell on the floor. Suzan noticed that one of the pictures was that of the old man with his wife and two children. Suzan got up, stunned, from her mother's bed and noticed that it is the same picture she saw in the old man's house on the wall. She asked her mother about the reason behind having this picture. Sara had no answer. She told her, "I think this old box belongs to your father, but I don't know anything about it. He did not let me know his personal things. Now my dear, we have to get some sleep Suzy. It was a long day."

Sara fell asleep but Suzan remained thinking about the reason behind having that picture.

The next day, her father came, who was always busy in traveling from one place to another to prepare stuff he needed in his factory. He came once each month, only to see his daughter and his other twin boys but regarding Sara, their relationship was not so well. At first he began as a simple worker, he learned much from his work in the old man's factory. Then, step by step he became professional in managing people. He was a really hard worker. Suzan always described him that way.

When he came home, and saw his daughter unable to go to school he advised her that she had to take some rest and never go outside her bed till she regains her health again. For that reason, he went to school to ask her for a sick leave. When she woke up she felt that she was still not fine but somehow able to struggle and complete her aim of saving Kris. She got out of the bed and suddenly felt better and was able to eat and walk. After that, she went out of the house to complete her mission and to tell the neighbours that they have to help Kris in preparing the required materials.

For that reason, she and the closest neighbours began to train him stealthily, in order not to make his grandfather know about it. As they also did not like the old man they began helping Kris by asking him about strange looking plants or kinds of flowers or other things that the committee may ask in the contest. They would carry out these exercises when he would come to the neighbourhood for the sake of visiting his grandfather. This took many days to memorize that various topics about plants, until the day of the competition.

The contest day was a very gloomy day, when it seemed that it would rain and darkness was becoming more. It was probably that a storm will come. The sky was full of dark clouds. This was unlike of what was happening inside the competition hall. Everything was so beautiful and glamorous. Flowers were decorated everywhere with their marvellous fragrant and students were eagerly waiting for the competitors to come and to stand before the committee. Suzan was not there, it could because of the weather. Kris wondered about her absence. Sometime later, she showed up but she seemed tired. She was very excited to see how the competition would start and how would Kris would do. Everything was good and the competitors began to answer the questions including Kris. As any concerned person , Suzan felt stressed in this situation.

She was shaking her legs and her thumb was on her teeth and she tried to encourage him in spite of her illness. Throughout the contest, Suzan noticed that Kris sometimes seemed happy and at times, he looked cold as if he was without feelings or his mind was full of many thoughts. *He has that kind of look that really frightens me. I do not know why but maybe it's just a feeling,* Suzan thought. The questions were starting to become harder but Kris confidently answered them all. The whole contest depended on giving marks to the contestants till finals. Those who collect more points will be nominated. After the nomination, there will be an exam for the first three contestants who got higher marks. When Kris was answering any question, Suzan was clapping with excitement till her hands became really red. After finishing most of the questions, they reached the final level. One of the rules of the contest was that if anyone made a mistake, it would lessen his/her marks and consequently the chance of winning and having that vacant job would be lost.

At last, the final question was directed to each one of the contestants. Suzan was excited to know what would happen. The weather outside started to rain. One of the committee member asked Kris about the same category he asked other contestants about, also around two kinds of flowers. Kris seemed so confidant as flowers were his specialty, till the question came! It was about lily and jasmine flowers. Kris seemed shocked. His eyes are full of tears and anger. His confidence was gone. He gazed at them all with anger as if he was remembering the whole disaster of that night when his two little sisters died. Unconsciously, he left the stage and ran away. Suzan followed him quickly till she reached him and a real argument happened between them. She was carrying an umbrella under the heavy rain. "Please Kris, do not lose everything." She was trying to convince him coming back to finish the competition.

He said, "Lose everything? To lose what more than I've lost; I was responsible for their death. How I could do this? How could I even think that I will complete my life easily!"

"Kris, you are not responsible for anything that happened. Your grandfather caused all this," she replied.

"What? What are you saying?" he said that mockingly.

"Yes, Kris. He was responsible for that disaster and he always makes you feel guilty all these long years. What happened was not your fault; it was his. He was controlling you, because he is obsessive with controlling everything."

Kris said in a sarcastic tone, "What? This is absurd, what are you saying?"

"Yes Kris, this is the truth. Your grandfather was responsible for leaking lethal gas when you both were outside your village. This made your sisters dead and also your father."

She continued, "He did all that. He…" She wanted to complete but Kris interrupted her with a loud voice, "Is that what your parents had lied to you?"

"My parents??? What is their relation with this thing? What is wrong with you?" she answered.

"Ah kid you know nothing then," Kris said.

"Know what?" she was surprised.

From some distance, the old man appeared and said, "Enough" but no one recognized his appearance or even heard him.

"What is going on Kris? Please tell me?" she begged.

"Leave me alone. I have to go." He got nervous.

He turned his back and was about to leave. At this moment, the weather became worse. Wind blew strongly, and it became colder.

"Yes go, run, and hide behind all your sad memories. It is my fault that I did not take my father's advice to stay at home." He turned again and hit her umbrella. He became mad "Your father! Oh? How he seems a good man that vile, wicked person."

"My father? How dare you talking about my father? What do you even know about him?" Suzan said shivering.

He continued talking, "Always, my grandfather was telling me that everything happens for a reason, always advising me to be patient, to be wise, to believe. He paid his life teaching me those trivial lessons. He placed me in the farm to forget all about my anger and misery and kept me away from everyone around who knew everything about the story except you kid."

"What story?" Poor Suzan was crying. The old man was struggling to reach them quickly, but the wind and the rain prevented him. and darkness was heavy so he could not see well.

Kris talked in a sharp tone and told her. "You want to know the story, well then. The story of your father who made that fatal mistake or who knows maybe it was not a mistake when he put a large amount of prohibited ingredients with each other. An accident occurred and my little sisters, who were allergic to latex, died. All this happened because of him. My great uncle. Your genius father." He shouted mockingly.

Then reached the old man and slapped Kris and told him "You learned nothing from what I have spent my life on all these long years. Your mother's poisonous speech has gotten hold of you; my years of preaching went in vain." Then Kris left furiously.

The old man looked at Suzan and said, "I am sorry my dear. But I hate to say that I have told you to stay away from him."

Suzan suddenly became very pale. She gazed with her open big eyes at him as if she regretted all things that she had said and believed in, but said nothing. In a minute she began to remember everything again. Meantime, the old man was talking to her but she was absentminded. She began to understand what the old man meant by his words. The whole truth became clear to her. The old man gave her the umbrella and started walking back home. Suddenly, she startled and stopped walking. She remembered Kris's words. If her father is his uncle then that women she saw that day was her aunt and this old man then is her grandfather. She whispered "My dear grandfather" then immediately fainted.

The old man took her home with much difficulty under rain and gave her to her mother but said nothing. Two days later, Suzan was so sick and had a high fever. Sara thought it was because of the night before. But she was getting worse.

No one knew where the old man was in those two days. Then he appeared and tried to check up on Suzan. Sara did not allow him to enter and said with teary eyes, "It is all because of you." Even though he was prevented, still he pushed the door and shouted, "Where is she?"

They went to Suzan's room and immediately he noticed the ficus elastic plant and shouted, "She has an allergy from latex?"

Sara surprisingly answered. "Yes, she has."

He took the plant at once and threw it out from the window. Then, he rushed to take Suzan from bed. He asked Sara about the one who gave her that plant. She said, "Kris, as he told Suzan that this plant will make her feel better."

The old man closed his eyes with remorse, as he knew Kris real intention of revenge because Kris was expert enough to know that this plant was capable of harming her.

Then quickly took her to the hospital running with all the power he got. At the hospital, they at once put her in intensive care. The old man and the mother began to talk. Sara asked in fear "What is going on?"

The old man was putting his forehead on his two hands which was on his stick. Then started his words with "Sara what I am about to tell you is something hard. I don't want you to be worry. But now is time to know the truth." Then he told her the whole story gradually when they sat at the hospital chairs for hours. He began explaining, how her husband, his own son, was responsible for doing everything and even putting him in jail for ten years. He had accused him that he was responsible for that deadly incident.

Sara asked "How and why?"

He answered, "As you know, I was the owner of the factory that my son, your husband, was working in."

She told him "No, actually I was not. I never knew he was working in his father's factory."

He continued, "In jail, I tried hard to meet Kris. His father was always hitting him, and his mother, my silly daughter, was always carefree. She cared only about herself. As for Kris, he loved his two little sisters so much. After their death and his father also after them my daughter immediately got married to a very wealthy man, who did not want Kris' existence. With time, Kris became so gloomy and aggressive. Especially after preventing him to see his new little sisters from his step-father. After ten years, when I came out from prison, the first thing that I tried to do was to find him. Because I know that he insisted to seek his uncle who destroyed his life. He was full of vengeance. At that time, you moved from one place to another. I followed him to many places he went to, just to prevent him from what he intended to do."

Sara said, "The places we were in, right? As we moved a lot until we settled here." Then, she began remembering the day before ten years ago. "Yes, I do remember that day very well, it was the day when I knew about my pregnancy of my twin boys when Suzan was only 5 years old. I was so happy that night until his coming. He was so frantic and weird. He put some kind of a plant, I think it was, it was the same one that was in Suzan's room. He put it in front of him and gazed at it whole night and how he was laughing as if he accomplished something. He was mumbling 'yes I did it yes I did it.'"

The old man spoke, "This plant has latex, when he put a large amount of it with other ingredients; the disaster happened and did what he did. That's why Kris' sisters died. So, Kris wanted to pay back for what happen to them with Suzan who by coincidence seemed to have the same disease. I think it's the family genes. But how did Kris know about her allergy?" he inquired.

Sara said regretfully, "Suzan went to him once, to tell him about a contest that her school had announced and also to ask him for an advice concerning her allergy."

The old man asked "Then, why she did not came to ask me? She used to come to me. I prevented her more than one time to go there."

Sara answered with shame that it was her fault. "I believed what was said about you. My husband was always mentioning how cruel you were, I am sorry, how you were not accepting his opinions and not giving him enough money for living as he deserved. Although, he was an agronomist, but you treated him as an ordinary worker in your factory. I also remember that he mentioned something, made you shout at him and also fire him that day. What was this thing, sir? Do you remember?" Sara wanted to know.

He said, "How could I forget. Actually, I do remember it very well. He told me to change the factory in order to produce medical things to sell them in a high price, instead of producing perfumes of lily and jasmine which I was famous in selling them in a low price and not like what have been mentioned about me in newspapers. So, I became so furious because he knew that medical stuff was so dangerous and needed precautionary measures. Also, the fact that my factory was inside the village and not in its outskirts, that's what made the disaster happened. For that reason, I fired him because I have seen evil in his eyes."

Then, Sara said to assure his speech "Yes, he opened a factory after that in selling medical stuff in the most expensive prices and this is what made us have a real conversation, after that we split."

While they were still talking, the doctor hurried up to go to Suzan's room and a strange movement was happening.

"What is going on?"

The nurses told them that Suzan had entered a coma.

Sara screamed and the old man was in a deep shock.

"Please calm down everything will be all right." At this moment, Suzan was in a deep sleep for days. She again saw the two girls in a dream and told them, "I am coming with you angels, you come to take me right?"

"No we are not. You have to come back; you have a family waiting for you. They are now waiting for you. Wake up Rosy. Wake up."

The week after the contest announcement had passed. They pronounced the three first winners and Kris was one of them. He collected a large number of scores which made him qualified to participate in the exam.

At the hospital, Sara was crying and the old man was praying for their beloved child. Sara heard his praying and she thanked him for everything he did, since he did not leave them alone in this hard situation. Meanwhile, Suzan's father, Jack, showed up and came to see his daughter. When he reached, he saw his father face to face again after all these long years. They were looking at each other and Jack was shocked about his father being here. He knew nothing about the whole matter. Sara remained silent. They were just looking at each other thoughtfully. Here, Kris's mother, Juan, came furiously to blame her father of not finding Kris and to ask him about her son's existence. So, when she found her father (the old man), Suzan's mother and Jack there, she was taken aback. It was like a family gathering.

"You are here! What are you all doing here?" Juan asked Jack. He told her, "I am here because of my daughter; she is sick. What you are doing here?"

"I came to ask my father about Kris, he is not there on the farm."

"What farm?" Jack wondered and the old man was just watching. Sara was not satisfied about what was going on.

"Of course, you know nothing about us Jack, always you think about yourself. Others' lives mean nothing to you." Juan added.

Jack answered, "Are you mad, do not you see that my own child is in the hospital, and you do nothing but talk about something that happened ten years ago."

"Is that what you think Jack? It is only something that happened before ten years. Do you not understand what you have done; all of this is because of you. You destroyed my family, you killed my two little girls, and you made my son miserable and desolated." Juan replied.

The old man said, "Enough, this is not the right time or place to talk about it Juan."

She continued accusing jack, "And what about your father, did you think about him? Did you ever blamed yourself about what you did to him? You put him in jail, what he did to you to treat him like that? How could you do this to him?" They all seemed irritated.

Then, Sara talked to Juan, "And you, your son tried to harm my daughter. What is her guilt to do this to her? she tried to help him."

Juan said with gloating, "I think that is fair. I always talked to Kris not to give up on his right, and that what he was always trying to do but my father was preventing him, he was always keeping an eye on his granddaughter to protect her. When I saw her that day in your house father, I hated her. She looks like her father. She reminds me of him. Now my father, I need to know where Kris is."

At that moment, the old man began to talk. He sat on the chair, "There is no difference between you and your brother, both of you harm your beloved ones. All of these years, I tried hard to convince Kris to let go of what had happened, to begin a new life, to start a new beginning and to stand up again. You, Juan, were always poisoning his mind with vengeance. So, I tried to keep you away from him, but I could not. When you were always coming to bring Kris different things like clothing, money, and other things, you were not doing it out of love, you needed to be near to him to poison his mind with all your bad thoughts. You create a monster. I congratulate you; you unfortunately win. I also wanted to tell you that your son is now in a mental hospital to be treated well and to make him, get rid of all those bad things inside his mind." Then a nurse came to tell them that Suzan is awake.

....

"After ten years, I stand here my lovely students to tell you that this story was about me. Your Herbology teacher. When I was your age, fifteen, I really loved that year in spite of my sickness. Yet, it was still a special year. What I have learned from through my life, now I convey it to you."

"So miss... miss... miss, please, Miss. Rosalina," said a student.

"Yes, Simon. I was absent minded," said Miss Rosalina.

"Why did you not mention your name from the beginning? And the letters on the woven hat mean what and..." The student tried to ask more questions but Miss Rosalina answered, "Wait, Simon, I will answer all of your questions one by one. First of all, I did not mention my name because, I wanted you to listen. Not just to know my story so you will be excited and attended. I wanted to teach you the most important lesson in your lives as well as it was in mine is that how to listen to things that you suppose to listen to. "

"What do you mean miss? You mean your Grandpa? When he told you that you have not to come alone to the farm. And you have to stay away from Kris?" said Simon.

"You are so clever Simon. That is true," said Miss Rosalina.

"But Miss Rosalina, what about the argument between the old man and Kris in the farm?" asked another one.

She said, "That is a good question too. It was about me actually. That's how Kris had to stay away from me and not to harm me. It was about my grandpa's insistence to convince Kris to let it go."

"You did not also mention about those two days of your grandpa's absence." students began asking as there were affected by her story.

"Yes, he took Kris during those two days to the mental hospital and after that, he came quickly to see me." She answered. "Now, miss, we understand the dream when you said 'wake up Rosy' we thought you made a mistake. But actually you were telling about your dream." One student commented.

"So, miss what about Kris' woven hat, what does it mean those letters?"

One of the students answered "I think the first letters of his two sisters L. J."

Another one asked, "What about the letter R?"

Miss Rosalina smiled and said, "I am proud of you all. It seems that you were good listeners," then added, "as for the woven hat, it means Lily, Jasmine and me, when I was five years old, I was just about Kris's twin sisters age. He made that hat from flowers as we all refer to roses at that time my father sometimes was taking me with him to the factory. I remember we were playing outside the factory. We loved each other so much although we did not know that we were a real family, but unfortunately my father made us apart and we lost connection with them."

"So, miss. I think the picture you saw in your grandfather's house meant Jack and Juan your father and your aunt and for reason you found it in your mother's room. Am I right miss?" Miss Rosalina clapped strongly and replied, "That is so right and precise."

"Miss Rosalina."

"Yes, Sarah?"

"What about the contest, Kris is supposed to have an examination."

"Very good, this is a good note," said Miss Rosalina. "When I woke up, my mother was crying and my grandfather was so happy. After coming back home, and knowing everything, the school made contact with us in order to tell Kris about the exam. But after explaining what had happened, they assured my grandfather to be the teacher of herbology as a reward to him."

"I forget to tell you my students that my beloved grandfather was the one who gave me that flower in the doormat of the house each time and not Kris as I thought. He knew this one was my favourite. He was watching me from a distance to make sure that I was well. He always wanted Kris to communicate with people, but Kris faced real problems in doing that. So for that he isolated him hoping to find inner peace."

Her students thanked her for sharing her story. They all told her, "Now we understand that we have to be careful judging others and not to believe anything said about anyone."

She said, "Yes, that is true. My grandfather was kept in jail unlawfully. People treated him as guilty. Newspapers ruined his reputation. Neighbours said unfair things about him. All these things happened because of unreal facts. And we all around him believed what is said about him."

"So, my great wonderful students, I shared this story with you for a reason. I want to tell you that, all my life I did not ever regret doing good to anyone, as I do believe that good will return to you back. But this time it will back in a better way. The impact of words is so powerful, and I myself will always keep on watching myself in saying anything, because my words could save someone's soul or it could be like an arrow in his heart. Always, we need to be careful in choosing our words."

"Those who hold flowers remain always fragrant, this is written on the grave stone of the old man."

"I thank you a lot my grandfather for everything and I need to tell you that. You are the one who thought me the real meaning of the impact of words."